The Magic Key

Fraser the Eraser

OXFORD

UNIVERSITY PRESS

D0543295

Gran was busy drawing a picture for Kipper when Mum called out to them that tea was ready.

Floppy was hungry and wanted to go inside for his tea. But Kipper grabbed him and pulled him back – he needed Floppy to pose for the picture. Gran held up the picture to show Kipper, but he wasn't happy.

'It's not the tree I saw in my head,' he said. 'It had different branches, and I wanted sea, not a river.' He stamped his feet and waved his arms. 'Why can't I get you to draw what I want you to draw?' he cried.

I wish he could, thought Floppy. I'm starving.

The key on Floppy's collar started to glow.

Suddenly, Gran, Kipper, and Floppy were whisked into a vortex of wonderful colours and lights. They were spinning round and round, faster and faster . . .

They found themselves on a sunny beach.

Kipper looked around excitedly. 'This is exactly the picture I wanted, Gran,' he said.

They heard a voice shouting to them. 'Make way for the Yellow Fellow!' it said.

Suddenly a huge yellow crayon appeared and started whizzing up and down the sand, colouring it all in.

Lots more giant crayons appeared. The pink, blue, and green crayons were called Peter Pink, Sue Blue, and Charlene Green. Sue Blue wasn't happy.

'I'm always doing sky,' she moaned to Gran. 'Sky, sky, and more sky. Boring!'

But before Gran could reply the wind started to howl around them.
'Take cover!' cried Peter Pink. 'It's Fraser the Eraser!'

Kipper found an umbrella and put it up to shield them from the
wind and from the big, mean-looking eraser who was running around
rubbing everything out.

'Rub-a-dub, rub-a-dub, rub-a-dub-dub!' he yelled.

All the crayons ran away and hid.

Fraser was enjoying spoiling the crayons' world. First he rubbed out the sky and then he started rubbing out the trees!

A sudden gust of wind picked up Kipper and the umbrella, and they floated out over the sea. Kipper quickly turned the umbrella upside down and it landed in the sea like a boat. SPLASH!

The crayons had all hidden in a big crayon tin.

'I'll catch you, crayons!' Fraser shouted to them. 'Then I'll make you draw pictures for me to rub out every minute of the day!'

'You leave those crayons alone!' Gran told him.

Fraser the Eraser snarled at her. 'Right then, I'll catch you instead,' he said, grabbing her arm, 'and shut you up in my pencil case!'

'Let Gran go!' yelled Kipper, paddling like mad to get back to the shore.

Fraser just laughed. 'Make the crayons draw me something exciting to rub out. Then I'll let her go,' he said with a wicked smile.

Kipper and the crayons tried to think of ways they could rescue Gran.

'I know!' said Kipper. 'What if you draw something that can eat him up?'

'Like what?' ask Charlene Green.

'Like . . . like . . . a beast!' Kipper said excitedly.

Everyone thought this was a great idea.

But the crayons weren't too sure what a beast should look like. Kipper tried to describe one. 'It has a head,' he started, 'and a tail . . .'

'Like him, you mean!' said Peter Pink, pointing at Floppy.

And before Kipper could stop them, the crayons were busy drawing away. And soon they'd finished their picture – a huge Floppy!

Fraser the Eraser whizzed up to the picture and rubbed it out. 'That wasn't very exciting, was it?' he laughed. 'I want something exciting to rub out!'

Not very exciting, thought Floppy. What a nerve!

Kipper tried again to describe a beast to the crayons. 'Red woolly fur, and shiny green eyes,' he said. 'Long yellow pointy teeth and twirly orange ears. And sharp pink claws!'

The crayons set to work and soon they had drawn a beast – and this time he was just right!

Fraser the Eraser came back but this time the beast chased him away.

'Fraser will rub him out,' sighed Sue Blue. 'He rubs out everything except my sea.'

Then Kipper had an idea. 'Maybe he doesn't like getting wet!' he said.

'If he gets wet,' cried Peter Pink, 'then he can't rub!'

The beast had finally caught Fraser and he was trapped between the beast's huge pink claws.

'Quick, Sue,' cried Kipper. 'Draw some rain.'

Sue Blue flew across the sky drawing huge, wet, raindrops. Soon Fraser was soaked.

'Oh no!' he cried. 'Please stop it! I'll only rub out what you don't want. I promise!'

'What if they promise to draw something for you to rub out every day?' Kipper suggested.

'Then I'll leave their world alone,' gulped Fraser.

The crayons cheered as Kipper went to fetch Gran. Peter Pink handed Kipper the umbrella. 'A little something to keep you and Gran dry!' he said.

Kipper looked at Floppy. 'The key's glowing,' he said.

We're going, thought Floppy.

Back in the garden Gran held up a new picture to show Kipper.
'That's just right, Gran,' he said.
'Well, once you told me exactly what you wanted, I could draw it,' replied Gran.

Kipper added the little umbrella to the picture. Perfect!

Just then, Mum called to them, 'Your tea's getting cold!'

I'm out of here, thought Floppy and ran into the house.

Gran and Kipper laughed. 'Wait for us!' called Gran, and they followed Floppy in.

OXFORD
UNIVERSITY PRESS

Great Clarendon Street, Oxford OX2 6DP

Oxford University Press is a department of the University of Oxford.
It furthers the University's objective of excellence in research, scholarship,
and education by publishing worldwide in

Oxford New York

Auckland Bangkok Buenos Aires Cape Town Chennai
Dar es Salaam Delhi Hong Kong Istanbul Karachi Kolkata
Kuala Lumpur Madrid Melbourne Mexico City Mumbai Nairobi
São Paulo Shanghai Taipei Tokyo Toronto

British Library Cataloguing in Publication Data available
ISBN 0-19-272451-7
3 5 7 9 10 8 6 4 2
Printed in Great Britain